TOKYO
DIGS A
GARDEN

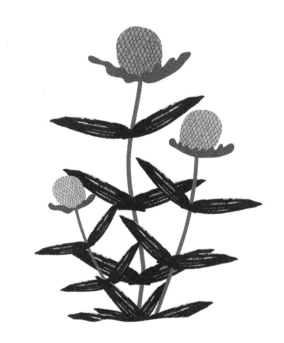

JON-ERIK LAPPANO

pictures by

KELLEN HATANAKA

GROUNDWOOD BOOKS   HOUSE OF ANANSI PRESS   TORONTO   BERKELEY

TOKYO lived with his mother, his father, his grandfather and a cat named Kevin in a small house that stood among tall buildings.

Tokyo's grandfather had lived in the small house since he was a boy. He loved to tell stories of how things used to be.

Then, the house looked over hills and forests and meadows and streams. Deer grazed on the hills. Foxes ran through the forests. Birds sang in the meadows. Salmon leaped from the streams.

But now, all of that was gone.
Tokyo's grandfather said the city had
eaten it all up.
Cities had to eat something, after all.

One sunny spring afternoon, Tokyo and Kevin were playing on the doorstep when they heard the music of an ice-cream truck.

Kevin jumped quickly over the gate.

Kevin loved ice cream.

But when they got to the street, they saw that there was no ice-cream truck at all — just an old cart, pulled by an old bicycle, pedaled by an even older woman. The cart was not full of ice cream. It was full of dirt.

Kevin was very disappointed.

The old woman held out her hand. She was holding three seeds.

"Plant these seeds," said the old woman. "And they will grow into whatever you wish."

She dropped the seeds into Tokyo's hand and continued along the road. Tokyo shrugged, put the seeds into his pocket and followed Kevin back to the house.

At lunch, Tokyo put the seeds on the table.

Grandfather looked at the seeds. Then he looked up at the small piece of sky peeking out between the tall buildings.

"Today is a good day for planting," he said.

Tokyo gulped down his glass of water, pretending he was a city drinking up a deep, cold lake.

Tokyo went into his backyard where nothing was growing. Not even a weed.

He looked at the ground and wondered where to plant the seeds. A little bug crawled slowly across the bricks before disappearing into a crack.

Tokyo had an idea. He lifted a brick, and underneath was cool, sandy soil. He made three holes with his finger, dropped one seed into each, and quietly made his wish. Then Tokyo covered the seeds with dirt.

That night, Tokyo dreamed he was riding an old bicycle through the city. All of a sudden, he turned into a fox, and the buildings changed into tall creaking pines.

Kevin dreamed of ice cream.

The next morning, Tokyo heard a bird singing.
When he peeked out his window, he saw three small
wildflowers sprouting up from the bricks in the middle
of the yard.

He ran to tell his grandfather. But when he got to
the kitchen, Grandfather was already staring out the
window in disbelief.

"*Neh*," said Grandfather, shaking his head. "I've never
seen anything grow that fast."

And Tokyo's garden kept growing.

After breakfast, the bricks around the flowers were completely covered with soft, spongy moss.

By dinner, three trees had grown, and the moss had become a meadow of wildflowers and shrubs.

By the next morning, the garden had grown up and over the buildings, across the street, down the road, over the cars and into the expressway.

The day after that, huge trees towered over apartments.
Their strong roots broke the pavement. Vines climbed
skyscrapers. Water poured from hydrants, flooding the
streets and turning them into rivers.

The day after that, the city was completely wild.
Deer foraged in office lobbies.
Rabbits burrowed under library carpets.
Bison stampeded through traffic lights.
Bears climbed telephone poles to search for honey
where bees had made their hives.

Tokyo, Grandfather and Kevin lay on their backs in the yard, which was now in the middle of a deep, dark forest.

"This garden is much too big," said Grandfather, shaking his head. "The cars can't drive because the streets are full of jumping salmon. Your mother had to take the old rowboat to work today. And there was a sloth in the elevator at your father's office so he had to take the stairs. What are we going to do?"

Tokyo thought for a moment. Kevin's tail twitched. A pack of monkeys swooped from branch to branch in the canopy above.

"I think," said Tokyo, "that we will just have to get used to it."

Grandfather watched a flock of cranes flying across the small piece of sky peeking out between the trees. He remembered how as a young boy he would watch them flying overhead before winter settled in.

"I think maybe you are right," he said.

Gardens have to grow somewhere, after all.

For Stephanie, who dreamed of our garden,
and for Maia and Amelia, who play in it
— JEL

In memory of Mary & Frank
— KH

•

Groundwood Books / House of Anansi Press
110 Spadina Avenue, Suite 801, Toronto, Ontario M5V 2K4
or c/o Publishers Group West
1700 Fourth Street, Berkeley, CA 94710

We acknowledge for their financial support of our publishing program the Canada Council for
the Arts, the Ontario Arts Council and the Government of Canada.

Canada Council   Conseil des Arts
for the Arts   du Canada

ONTARIO ARTS COUNCIL
CONSEIL DES ARTS DE L'ONTARIO
an Ontario government agency
un organisme du gouvernement de l'Ontario

With the participation of the Government of Canada
Avec la participation du gouvernement du Canada   Canadä

Library and Archives Canada Cataloguing in Publication
Lappano, Jon-Erik, author
Tokyo digs a garden / written by Jon-Erik Lappano;
illustrated by Kellen Hatanaka.
Issued in print and electronic formats.
ISBN 978-1-55498-798-6 (bound). —
ISBN 978-1-55498-799-3 (pdf)
I. Hatanaka, Kellen, illustrator II. Title.
PS8623.A73745T65 2016   jC813'.6   C2015-903592-9
                                          C2015-903593-7

The illustrations were created digitally with watercolor,
ink drawings and collage.
Design by Kellen Hatanaka
Printed and bound in Malaysia

FSC
www.fsc.org
MIX
Paper from
responsible sources
FSC® C012700